FRED
The Mouse™
Rescuing Freedom
Book Three

Written by Reese Haller

Illustrated by Thomas Haller

PERSONAL POWER PRESS Inc.

Fred The Mouse ™
Rescuing Freedom
Book Three

Library of Congress Card Number
2006932351

ISBN - 13: 978-0-9772321-3-0
ISBN - 10: 0-9772321-3-1

Printed in the United States of America

Personal Power Press, Inc.
P.O. Box 547
Merrill, MI 48637

Cover Design
Foster & Foster, Inc.
www.fostercovers.com

Book Design
Connie Thompson, Graphics etcetera
connie2@lighthouse.net

DEDICATION

I dedicate *Fred the Mouse™ Book Three: Rescuing Freedom* to all the people of the world, past and present, who worked and continue to work to make freedom possible for me, my family, and the community in which I live. I appreciate my parents for teaching me the power of being able to choose and for supporting me in becoming who I desire to be right now.

Thank You.

Portraits by Gregg

MY MISSION

I want to touch the hearts and minds of millions of kids around the world and help them see that they don't have to wait until they are older to become who they want to be. They can start now. Through my presentations and book writing I hope to inspire kids everywhere to read and then write their own books. I plan on creating a library where all the books are written by kids for kids.

Visit Reese's Website: **www.reesehaller.com**

Portraits by Gregg

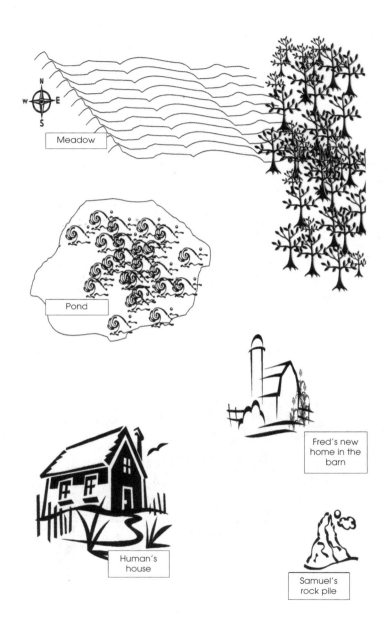

Meadow

Pond

Fred's new
home in the
barn

Human's
house

Samuel's
rock pile

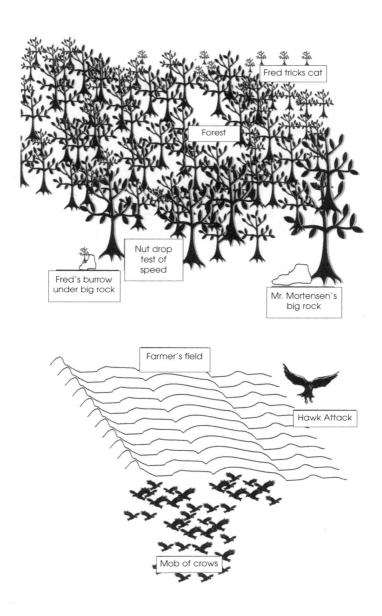

CONTENTS

Chapter 1

The Family Reunion

 "AAAAAAAAAAHHHH!"

An ear-piercing scream rang out as a bird swooped down on a large gathering of mice at the edge of the field. In the blink of an eye the bird descended from the clouds and landed in the middle of the unsuspecting mice below.

As soon as the bird touched the ground the scream turned to laughter. "That was awesome," giggled a tiny voice as a young field mouse climbed down from the barn swallow's back. "Mama, Mama, did you see me? I was up in the clouds!"

"Yes, I saw you, dear," replied the mama mouse.

"I want to go again," squeaked the young mouse, full of excitement.

"Maybe later. Let's give Mr. Lou a rest," said Mama Mouse. "Go play with your cousins over by the big rock."

The young mouse started to whine, "Do I have to? I want another ride."

A deep voice interrupted the whining. It was Brittney's father. "Brittney Anne, you heard your mother. Scurry off."

Brittany Anne frowned. "Yes Papa," and she slowly turned in the direction of the big rock.

"I think I saw your Uncle Fred over there, honey. He was telling stories again," added Mama Mouse.

With that Brittney Anne was off in a flash, yelling, "Uncle Fred! Uncle Fred! Uncle Fred!"

Brittney Anne's mama was correct. Fred was over by the big rock surrounded by dozens of little mice. He was telling the story of how he became a scurry and scamper champion and how he learned to trust his intuition, sensing danger just before it happened.

Brittney Anne became quiet as she got closer. Uncle Fred was talking.

"I remember the first time I felt the tightening of my tummy that tells me danger is near. It was at the Scurry and Scamper School," said Fred.

"Do we get to go to that school, too?" interrupted a voice from the middle of the crowd of mice.

"Oh yes," replied Fred. "All the mice in this area get to attend the Scurry and Scamper School. It is important that you all learn how to keep yourself safe out there in the field."

"Tell us more about the first time you felt your tummy tighten, Uncle Fred," came another small voice from the crowd.

"Yes, back to my story. I was just a few weeks older than you when I entered the

Scurry and Scamper School. I was learning the art of scampering like everyone else. My dad, your Great Uncle Arthur, taught me a song. It goes like this:

First you put your nose up,
Sniff, sniff.
Then you put your ears out,
Twitch, twitch.
Open up your eyes,
Blink, blink.
Then we scurry and scamper.

"That song helped me stop, think, and feel before I ran off. As I sang the song I could feel my stomach tingle or get real tight and cramp. I learned that the cramping feeling was my body telling me that danger was near. That one skill has helped me stay out of danger many times."

Fred stopped talking for a moment and then took a deep breath. "Have you ever been doing something that you knew you should not be doing and you get a feeling inside that tells you that it's wrong and you should stop?" Fred looked out at the faces of his nieces and nephews to see if his words were making sense. Some of the mice were nodding their heads yes.

He continued, "That feeling inside tells you that you shouldn't be doing that activity and you should make a different choice and do the right thing. That feeling is your intuition."

Again Fred paused and looked closely at the young faces staring at him. Their heads nodded again as if to show they understood what he was talking about.

Fred continued, "Let me tell you about the first time I had a strong feeling that danger was near. It was during the final exam at the Scurry and Scamper School. They called it the "Test of Senses." I started down a long dark tunnel when all of a sudden my tummy tightened and I thought I smelled something. But I didn't understand what I was smelling. Many strange scents came together all at the same time. For a moment I thought I could smell hawk and owl and snake and fox. Something just didn't feel right to me so I didn't go any further and I ran out of that hole as fast as I could. I learned from Mr. Mortensen that I had smelled the scent of danger. That feeling was my intuition telling me to stop and make a different choice."

The young mice were fixed on Fred's every word. With their mouths still hanging open, Fred continued, "You too will have many opportunities to learn about your intuition and how to trust your feelings."

Fred continued to talk about his scurry and scamper training when he noticed a familiar face that he had not seen in many months, not since leaving home in search of his dream. In the midst of the anxious young listeners stood Fred's cousin, Frank.

Fred stopped his storytelling in midsentence, shouted, "Frank!" and began to run through the crowd of tiny mice.

"Fred, old boy, long time no see," chimed Frank as the two cousins embraced.

After a brief hug Fred turned to his attentive audience

"Let's take a break. I can tell you more stories later. Everyone run off to the field for a little scurry and scamper practice."

With a few moans and groans, Fred's young nieces and nephews slowly dispersed and one by one disappeared among the dirt clumps at the field's edge.

Frank quickly continued, "I heard you found your dream and are creating a peaceful new home."

"Yes," replied Fred. "I have a bunch of new friends who are all different and yet very much the same."

"Is it true that your best friend is a snake?" interrupted Frank.

"Oh, you mean Samuel. I do spend a lot of time with Samuel. He is a wise old garter snake who seems to know about everything," commented Fred.

"Well," continued Frank "I think I would like to talk to him too. I want to know more about living in the city."

"Living in the city? You're a field mouse. What do you know about living in the city?" Fred questioned him in astonishment.

"Not much and I want to check it out anyway. I have the freedom to choose where I want to live and I'm thinking about moving inside for the winter and becoming a house mouse," said Frank calmly.

"Okay. First thing tomorrow morning we'll head to Samuel's house. He doesn't get moving until the sun is high in the sky. I can show you around my new home and introduce you to some of my other friends until he wakes up," replied Fred.

"Sounds good," chimed Frank. "I'll meet you back here first thing tomorrow." There was a brief pause as the two exchanged glances and nodded. Then Frank continued, "Come on. Let's go check out the nut-n-berry buffet. I heard it's the best."

The two cousins scurried off in the direction of the buffet, chatting as they went. Little did they suspect that valuable lessons about freedom were soon to appear in their lives.

Chapter 2

Back Home

 The sun rose gently over the field's edge and lightly touched the tiny drops of dew clinging to the grass and leaves near the ground. Fred had fallen asleep shortly after filling his belly at the nut-n-berry buffet. He was not used to being up at night any more.

Fred's sleeping habits had changed since moving out and creating a new life in the field where he was born. All of Fred's new friends, a barn cat named Tar, the family dog named Tiffany, Lou and Lou, the two barn swallows, Maggie the crow, Mortequie the turtle, and of course Samuel, were all awake and very active during the day. So Fred slowly gave up his nocturnal ways to join his friends during the daylight hours.

The sun glistening through the tiny beads of dew fell upon Fred's face as he crawled out from under a large oak leaf. He yawned, stretched his legs, and quickly scanned his surroundings in search of any of his relatives from the night before. It was clear that a party had taken place. Nut shells and half-eaten berries were everywhere, but there was no sign of any mice.

Fred figured that everyone was probably asleep for the day so he quietly made his way to the big rock where he planned to meet Frank.

Fred rounded the south edge of the rock and was startled to see Frank pacing back and forth.

"Good morning, Fred," blurted Frank in excitement.

"Wow, Frank, have you been waiting long?" asked Fred.

"I don't know, probably felt longer than it actually was," replied Frank.

"Well, then, let's not keep you waiting any longer," said Fred. "Follow me."

But before Fred stepped out from behind the protection of the big rock he focused his feelings. He took a deep breath, thought about the song his father taught him, and then checked out his feelings inside. His tummy felt calm. He looked into the sky. It was clear. He listened carefully. The air was still. He sniffed and waited.

Frank remained still, even in his excitement. He knew of Fred's intuitive ability. He was there the day Fred was crowned the scurry and scamper champion. He wasn't going to move a muscle, no matter how excited he was, until Fred gave the signal.

Within seconds Fred nodded, and off the two dusty brown mice ran, weaving along the field's edge. Fred stopped several times to check for safety. Each time Frank waited patiently. Each time the two continued in a weaving pattern until their destination was reached.

Upon arrival at the barn Fred yelled out, "Lou! Lou!"

Frank stood with his mouth hanging open "You live in here?"

"Well not all of it. I mostly live under that part over there," Fred replied motioning with his paw at the green door that led into the tack room. Months ago Fred had created a cozy home under the boards of the tack room just after the barn was built.

Frank wandered towards the doors still staring in awe, when Lou suddenly land- ed next to him and said, "Hi, Fred." Startled, Frank screamed and fell to the ground in fright.

Fred quickly ran to Frank's side. "It's okay, Frank. This is Lou, my barn swallow friend I was telling you about."

Frank was breathing heavily and clutching his chest with his front paws. "I know you said that you had a couple of friends that were birds, but I wasn't ready to suddenly have one standing next to me."

"Oh, I'm sorry," interjected Lou softly. "I didn't mean to startle you. For a moment there I thought you were Fred. You look just like him."

"This is my cousin, Frank," said Fred as Frank continued to breathe heavily.

"Pleased to meet you," said another voice from behind Frank.

Frank jumped and spun about frantically. Behind him stood another barn swallow that looked exactly like the first. Frank's head flipped back and forth between the two birds as he blurted out, "Stop doing that!"

"Come on, guys. Give Frank a break. No more sneaking up on him and playing your double-bird game," said Fred in an attempt to rescue Frank. Fred continued, "Frank, this is Lou," pointing to the bird on the right. "And this is Lou," pointing to the bird on the left.

"Pleased to meet you," they both said in unison.

"It's confusing enough that you both look alike, and then you have the same name, too," stammered Frank, who was beginning to regain his composure.

"Yeah, we get that a lot," replied the Lou on the right.

"Come on, let's go flying," interrupted the Lou on the left.

"That's a great idea," said Fred. "I can show Frank the lay of the land and all around my new home from up there."

"Uuhhhh . . . I - I - I don't know," stammered Frank.

Fred quickly interrupted "Frank, it's the fastest way into the city and there is no time like the present to learn. Later we can have Maggie take you into the city. He

knows his way around. Climb on like this."

Fred demonstrated the proper bird-mounting technique as Lou lowered his head. Within seconds Fred was aboard, sporting a gigantic smile. Frank took a deep breath and mounted the barn swallow just the way Fred showed him. He too was aboard in seconds.

"Hang on!" yelled Lou, and off the two barn swallows flew.

As usual, Fred giggled loudly. He loved the tingly feeling he got in his stomach every time he left the ground. He called it "the tummy tickle." Frank's tummy tingled too, but he gritted his teeth, closed his eyes, and hung on tighter as Lou rose higher in the sky.

Several minutes of gentle gliding helped Frank get accustomed to the feelings of flight. When Frank opened his eyes they were circling near the clouds. Flying next to him on the other Lou, smiling from ear to ear, was Fred.

"Look over there. You can see the big rock where we were this morning. And over there is the pond where my friend Mortequie lives. Down there is where the humans live. Hey, I can see Tiffany, the family dog, in the backyard."

Frank was amazed at how far he could see and how easy it was to spot any movement on the ground. As they flew, he imagined being a bird soaring through the sky searching for his next meal. "Hawks can spot us moving from up here with very little effort," Frank thought to himself. "No wonder so many mice are missing every year."

Fred was still rambling on, pointing out various landmarks while Frank remained fixed on his thoughts. He was enjoying the feeling of having the wind blow through his fur and the tingling of his whiskers as the air rushed past his face. He was amazed at how Lou seemed to move so freely and flow with the air currents. "Oh, a bird's world is so much larger than that of a mouse. Birds are able to fly to the city and back so easily. A journey that would certainly take a mouse days or even weeks," he thought to himself. He didn't hear much of what Fred was saying as he remained deep in thought. He was becoming more certain that his decision to move into the city was the right choice for him.

Frank's thoughts were interrupted by Fred shouting, "Frank - Frank - Look down there by those rocks. Samuel is up early today!"

Sure enough, Frank could see a snake curled up on a flat rock on the south side of an enormous pile of rocks.

"Let's go," shouted Frank.

"Hang on," yelled Lou as the two barn swallows dove towards the ground. This sudden movement gave Fred and Frank the tummy tickle. Fred giggled and Frank gritted his teeth. Seconds later, Lou and Lou alighted next to Samuel.

Chapter 3

Frank Meets Samuel

Fred and Frank jumped from the backs of their flight companions and stepped closer to Samuel.

"Greetings-s-s, young mice," Samuel began. "I s-s-see you have brought s-s-someone with you, Fred." His tongue was flickering in and out as he tasted the air. "The s-s-scent in the air indicates-s-s that he is-s-s a family member. A cousin perhaps-s-s?"

Frank stood motionless. He had never been this close to a snake before. And this snake had figured out, in seconds, who he was.

"Yes, Samuel. This is my cousin, Frank," replied Fred.

"Pleas-s-sed to meet you, Frank," nodded Samuel, his tongue still flickering wildly.

"H-h-hello," stammered Frank.

"S-s-sit, enjoy the s-s-sun's-s-s energy. Be s-s-still. S-s-soon we can talk. First let's-s-s just be together in quiet reflection."

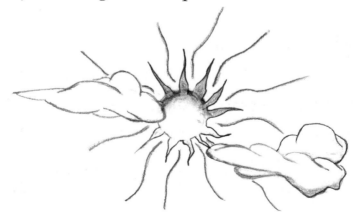

Fred was familiar with this custom. It was Samuel's way, to begin each day in quiet reflection. Fred had joined Samuel almost daily throughout the summer. He had come to appreciate this quiet time and looked forward to the peace it brought.

Frank watched Fred closely and followed his every move. His mind was racing with the questions he had been wanting to ask this wise old snake since he had first heard of him a few months ago from Fred's sister, Alyssa.

At first it was difficult for Frank to sit still and concentrate on being calm. He just wanted to get to his questions. He wanted answers. He felt so close and yet so far. As he sat his mind slowly stopped racing and his questions seemed to vanish. His body began to feel warm, and a small voice penetrated the silence. It was Samuel.

"Now that you are calm and your mind is clear, what is-s-s it you wish to know?" Samuel asked calmly.

Frank opened his eyes and looked at Samuel "I have the freedom to live wherever I want and I think I want to move to the city, but I'm not sure. How will I ever find a place to live? Will I be able to handle being a house mouse?"

"You already know," replied Samuel softly. "The answer is-s-s within you. S-s-sit quietly for a few moments-s-s longer and remain open to what is-s-s within you. Don't try to find the answer. Let it come to you."

Frank closed his eyes again and did as Samuel suggested. He sat and sat and sat. Then he thought he smelled something in his imagination. It was an aroma that had never entered his nostrils before. In his mind he saw the scent oozing from a small crack at the base of a big house. A sense of peace settled into his body and for some reason he smiled.

Samuel, who sensed Frank's peacefulness, tapped Fred on the shoulder with the tip of his tail and nodded in Frank's direction.

"What is it, Frank?" asked Fred.

"I know what I am looking for. I don't know if I can describe it, but I'll know it when I feel it," replied Frank, still smiling.

"Thank you for your help. I feel confident I can make the right choice for me."

"Maggie usually s-s-stops-s-s by in the late afternoon," said Samuel. "He might give you a ride into the city then. In the meantime tell me more about yourself, Frank."

The three sat in the warm summer sun talking about family, friendship, and the search for dreams. Frank learned that Samuel was a vegetarian and had chosen to leave home at an early age because his family had difficulty accepting his different eating preferences. Samuel answered as many of Frank's questions about humans and the city as he possibly could.

The day passed quickly and it wasn't long before Maggie arrived just as Samuel had promised.

Chapter 4

The Subdivision

 Maggie's large black-feathered body towered over Fred, Frank, and Samuel as the four companions sat in the hot summer sun. Frank had heard of Maggie, more formally known as Maggilicutty, the leader of the Mob of Crows.

It was Maggie's mob that had participated in the Mouse Scurry and Scamper School's final exam. The Mob of Crows, with Maggie as their powerful leader, enjoyed working at the school pretending to be hawks and owls during the final test of a mouse's scurry and scamper abilities.

Every year the test, concluded with all the young students being required to scamper across the farmer's field without being captured by the crows. Every year Maggie and the Mob took great pride in capturing all the young mice and returning them to Mr. Mortensen, the school principal, for additional scurry and scamper training. Those who were caught by the crows had to return for several more weeks of lessons.

Only one mouse in the long history of the Mouse Scurry and Scamper School had returned to the school principal on his own, avoiding the crows capture. That mouse was Fred. Following his return Fred was crowned the scurry and scamper champion and his fame had spread throughout the entire region. Fred was famous to mouse and bird alike.

Maggie and Fred were now close friends and had spent hours together on flying adventures. Crow, with tiny mouse aboard, would fly to area fields or into the city creating endless adventures. Maggie knew the city well, and he agreed to take Fred and Frank to an area he called a "subdivision," where there would be lots of houses like the one Frank had imagined.

Before leaving, Maggie took time to sit quietly with Samuel as he frequently did in the late afternoon. While Samuel and Maggie sat together, Frank and Fred went in search of nuts and berries to take on their trip to the subdivision.

The two cousins returned an hour later with a small bag of goodies to find Maggie exactly where they had left him, sitting on the rock next to Samuel. Maggie asked Frank a few more questions about the house in his imagination and what he had experienced to get a clear idea of what group of houses might work best. Once clear about which direction to head in, Maggie nodded to Samuel and the two mice climbed onto his back. "See you tomorrow, Samuel," shouted Maggie as his powerful wings pumped the air, quickly lofting the three off the ground. Within seconds they were above the height of the trees.

"Wheeeee," shouted Fred. "That tickles my tummy every time. I love that feeling." Fred enjoyed the sense of freedom he got being able to fly and travel in the air.

Frank gritted his teeth and hung on tight. A few minutes passed before he opened his eyes. He looked over at Fred who was grinning from ear to ear.

"Look," said Fred. "You can see a bunch

of houses way over there."

Maggie shouted back over his shoulder, "I'm going to take you to that group of houses over there," motioning with his head to the right. "That's a large gathering of houses just outside the city area and I've heard that it is called a subdivision. One of my robin friends says there are about 75 houses down there. You ought to be able to find what you're looking for in that group."

Frank watched closely as Maggie started his descent and they moved in closer. The houses became bigger and bigger the closer they got. Maggie passed over several houses and then landed in the middle of a circle of houses. "This is about the center of the group," he said. "You can get to a bunch of houses rather quickly from here."

Fred jumped from Maggie's back and landed on a large patch of soft, plush green grass. Frank sat motionless with his mouth hanging open.

"Come on, Frank, let's go check things out," called Fred as he looked up at Frank.

"You guys spend the night poking around. I'll meet you back here tomorrow morning," said Maggie as Frank slid from his back.

"This way, Frank," motioned Fred while Maggie lifted off the ground and quickly took flight. The two mice slipped into the thick grass and disappeared from plain sight. Every now and again their brown bodies could be spotted popping over clumps of grass.

Their first stop was at the base of a red brick house. They took a moment to catch their breath and create a house-hunting plan. They leaned against the massive structure to think for a moment.

After a few minutes Frank broke the silence "I have an idea. I want to go to each house, lean against its base, like we're doing right now, close my eyes, and think calmly for a few minutes. That way I can check my feelings to see if they match what I felt earlier at Samuel's."

"I'll keep watch for you so you don't have to worry about any predators," suggested

Fred. "Let's start in that direction and move our way around to each house from this central point."

"Sounds good."

So the two set out to do just that. House after house, Fred would stand guard while Frank calmed his mind and body and checked out his feelings inside. Frank waited for a feeling, and when that feeling didn't match the feeling from Samuel's, the two would scurry to the next house.

Fred's ability to sense danger was extremely comforting to Frank. He knew he could fully concentrate on his inner feelings. He did not have to be concerned about any animals pouncing on him while deep in thought. He knew Fred would keep him safe. The mice spent the entire night running from house to house, repeating the pattern over and over again without saying a word to each other.

The darkness was giving way to the next day's light when Fred broke the silence "Maggie is going to be coming soon. We should start to head back."

"I want to check that old-looking house over there, and then we'll go back," replied Frank in a quiet voice. "I haven't found what I'm looking for yet."

"Okay," replied Fred and off they ran.

Fred reached the house first and stopped several feet from the base. He smelled something. It was an unfamiliar scent, and he froze in his tracks in surprise and puzzlement. He had not smelled that smell before.

Frank caught up to Fred and stopped next to him. "What's wrong Fr . . ."

But before he could finish his question, he too caught the scent. Immediately Frank closed his eyes and took a deep breath. "That's it. That's the smell, the one I had in my vision at Samuel's," he whispered. "Look around. Where is it coming from?"

Fred stood motionless, staring at Frank, who had a peaceful look on his face. Frank opened his eyes and looked at the corner of the house. "Look at that. It looks like smoke. That's the way in." After a brief moment of silence, he stated, "I'm going in!"

"Are you sure?" asked Fred.

"Yes," replied Frank quickly. "Come back in five days to check on me."

The determined look on Frank's face gave Fred no reason to question his cousin any further. He knew this is what Frank wanted to do. Fred followed Frank to the corner of the old brick house. Sure enough, a small crack appeared about two mouse-body lengths off the ground. Frank stuck his nose up to the crack "Yep, that smell is definitely coming from inside the house."

They both stood staring at the crack for a moment.

"Boost me up," said Frank confidently. "I'll see you back here in five days no matter what."

Fred put out his front paws and lifted Frank up. He watched him slip into the crack and disappear. Fred stood for a moment to see if Frank would return. When Frank didn't return, Fred turned and scurried off to meet Maggie in the center of the subdivision. Silently, he wondered, "Will I ever see Frank again?"

Chapter 5

The Stranger

 Five days later Fred was back waiting by the crack in the wall. He had asked Maggie to drop him off before sunrise so he wouldn't miss Frank in case he came out early. Fred had been waiting almost an hour, and his anxiety was building. Frank had been in that house for five days. Fred was worried. He was focusing on staying positive by repeating a phrase to himself while pacing back and forth. "Frank's a smart mouse. He can handle himself."

He kept repeating the phrase aloud as the hour passed "Frank's a smart mouse. He can handle himself."

"Frank's a smart mouse. He can handle himself."

"Frank's a smart mouse. He can handle himself."

"Hey, Fred, what are you doing?" giggled Frank as he stuck his head out of the tiny crack in the wall.

Startled, Fred spun around and shouted, "Frank, you're okay!"

"Of course I'm okay. C'mon, the morning meal is about to begin. You don't want to miss this. Follow me."

Frank reached out his paw. Fred grabbed hold and squeezed into the crack by making his body as thin as possible. Once inside, his nostrils filled with a magnificent aroma.

"Wow, what's that smell?" asked Fred.

"That's the smell I was telling you about," replied Frank. "That's the wonderful smell that helped me choose to be a house mouse."

"It sure does smell good. What is it?"

"The humans call it 'bacon and eggs.' I don't know what food is the bacon and what is the egg. I just know there is always a lot of it on the floor when they're done," commented Frank, with a small bit of drool forming in the corner of his mouth.

"C'mon," interrupted Fred "Let's go get some."

The two cousins were off in a flash. Together they scurried up the inside of the wall just under the kitchen and popped out a tiny hole in the back of a cupboard full of pots and pans.

"Watch your step," whispered Frank. "Some of these pans tip easily and make a huge racket. It gets the humans all worked up."

Frank carefully weaved his way through the pans, with Fred close on his tail. Slowly the two mice lowered themselves down a space in the front of the cupboard and onto the kitchen floor.

"Stay close to the wall and follow me," whispered Frank, barely making a sound. Fred nodded a silent reply.

Along the base of the wall they raced on their tiny legs as they both kept a close eye on every move the humans made. Not a single glance was made in their direction. The humans were focused on eating. Arms and hands flew everywhere as the sound of forks scraping plates filled the air.

When they reached the other side of the room, Frank stopped. "We'll wait here in the corner."

Huddled in the corner under a collection of potted flowers on a trilevel stand Fred could see the entire kitchen at a glance.

Frank had obviously done this before. Not only could Fred see the humans and their strange eating behavior but he could also see across the kitchen where they had just been a few minutes earlier and into the next room.

Frank's eyes seemed to stay focused on the floor by the humans' feet. He appeared to be marking each tiny piece of food as it hit the ground and remembering its location. Fred, on the other hand, was drawn to the adjoining room. He didn't know why, but he felt like something or someone was looking at him. Having learned to trust his inner feelings, he continued to scan the room with his eyes.

Several minutes passed, and the feeling of being looked at continued. Then he saw it and realized the feelings he was having were indeed accurate. A strange white creature appeared in the distance. "F-F-Frank, w-w-what's that?" whispered Fred with a hint of fear in his voice.

"What's what?" whispered Frank in a frustrated voice, while continuing to keep his eyes fixed on the food under the table.

Fred pointed to the other room and tapped Frank on the shoulder. "Look! Over there. Something is looking at us."

With that Frank turned and noticed the fig-ure in the other

room "I never saw that before. What is it?"

"You probably never noticed it because you were too busy listening to your stomach and looking at all the food," replied Fred. "Let's go check it out."

"The humans just started eating, and they won't notice us if we go now. We can't go food collecting until they leave the area anyway. So I guess now is as good a time as any," responded Frank.

Making their bodies as low to the ground as possible, the two mice scurried along the wall through the eating area and into the other room. The floor beneath their feet changed from a hard surface to a soft cushy one. They scampered under a long object that was low to the ground and easily blocked the humans' view of them. They popped out on the other side right below where they thought the creature was located.

Fred stopped to check his feelings. He wasn't sensing any danger, so he stepped out a little further and looked up. "I think it's up there."

Frank stepped out from under the structure and looked up, too. "Well, if you're not sensing any danger, let's go check it out. When we get to the top I'll keep an eye on the humans for you."

The soft cloth sides of the long structure they were under made it easy for their paws to grab hold. The climbing was easy, and within seconds they both stood atop the soft object. They gasped at what they saw. On a small table about four mouse-body lengths away stood a creature with red eyes and fur as white as snow. They froze.

Chapter 6

Confused

 The red-eyed creature looked back at them inquisitively but made no attempt to come closer or run away. It stood motionless, staring at Fred and Frank.

"What is it?" whispered Frank.

"I don't know. I'm having trouble smelling anything," replied Fred. "You keep an eye on the humans. I'm going over there."

Frank nodded "Be careful."

Fred took a few steps back and with a

short running start easily jumped the gap. His paws hit the surface on the other side and slid out from underneath him. His brown furry body slid easily across the slippery surface and came to an abrupt halt. Fred looked up. Standing directly in front of him was the white stranger. Fred jumped to his feet and found himself nose to nose with the stranger, except their noses were not touching each other. An invisible wall separated them. Fred stood up with his hind legs leaning against the invisible wall. The stranger also stood up and the two stared intently at one another.

Fred sniffed and could not get a direct smell of the stranger's body. He lowered his front paws and slowly walked around the seemingly invisible box, sniffing at the edges. The stranger followed his every move from inside the box. There appeared to be no way in and no way out. The stranger was in a cage.

Fred walked all the way around the structure and stopped back at the place where he had begun. He looked over at Frank who silently motioned up to the top of the glass box. Fred looked at the humans, then at Frank, and then up at the box. Guessing his thoughts, Frank quickly jumped the gap and slid next to Fred. "I'll boost you up," he whispered. Fred nodded and in one motion jumped on Frank's shoulders and then onto the lid of the cage.

From on top Fred could see the design of the cage. There was a dish of food in one corner, a water bottle hanging in another corner, and a wheel-like structure in the middle. The top was made of thin metal and had tiny holes in it. Fred could now smell the stranger below. "You smell like a mouse, but you don't look like any mouse I've ever seen," he said.

A soft voice replied, "Yes, I am a mouse. I'm a white albino mouse."

"I'm a field mouse. My name is Fred."

"I don't think I have a name. The humans just call me mouse."

"Are you trapped?" asked Fred.

"No, I live here," said the white mouse.

"How long have you been in here?" asked Fred.

The white mouse thought for a moment. "I've always lived in a space like this," she answered slowly.

"You're in a cage. How do you get out?"

questioned Fred in astonishment.

"I don't want to get out. This is my home," replied the white mouse.

"But you can't run free. Help me chew a hole in this part right here and I'll get you out," pleaded Fred.

"Why? I don't want out. I have everything I need right here. I have food brought to me everyday. I can get a drink whenever I want right over there. I can run in my wheel at any time. I'm warm and I'm safe. I have everything I want. I'm fine right here."

Fred was confused, completely puzzled. "You have everything you NEED, but you don't know what else is out there. You might want something different or some-thing more if you knew. You could have the entire outside world, to run and play in. You could be free."

"I am free enough," replied the white mouse.

"Fred," called Frank from below. "The humans are finishing up. We better get out of sight."

Fred called down to the white mouse who was now sitting in the opposite corner. "I'll come back so we can talk more." He jumped to the table. Frank joined him as they both jumped across the gap, then slid down the side of the soft structure and out of sight.

The two mice waited for the humans to clear the eating room before they made a dash to the other side of the kitchen. Once across the floor they slipped into the cupboard, ran across the pans, and headed for Frank's new nest. Frank slid down a wire and across a platform where his nest rested in the corner.

Once safely in Frank's nest, Fred spoke "I don't understand. With the white mouse's help I could chew a hole big enough for her to crawl through. In less than an hour she could be free. She refused to help. That mouse doesn't want to be free. I'm confused."

"Maybe the white mouse has never been free before and has no idea what it means," replied Frank.

"I think I have to talk to Samuel about this," commented Fred. "I'm going to head back to the barn. Maggie said he was going to be flying around the neighborhood all day and I can catch a ride back at any time. Are you coming?"

"No," replied Frank. "I'm going back inside to talk to the white mouse some more. I think if she only knew what it was like out here she would want to be out of that cage. I'll meet you back here tomorrow at sunrise."

Fred nodded and quickly scurried out the crack in the wall to find Maggie. He had some puzzling concerns about freedom and wanted to talk to Samuel.

Chapter 7

Understanding Freedom

From high in the sky on Maggie's back Fred could see Samuel's rock pile. How he hoped his wise old friend was awake and sunning on his rock. Fred could also see movement and commotion around the barn.

Maggie saw it, too. "It looks like the humans are out. I wonder what's going on."

As a precautionary measure Maggie circled the barn a few times to survey the situation. It looked like a new creature had arrived at the barn, a horse. The humans were taking care of the horse on the back side of the barn. Maggie carefully landed several feet from Samuel's rocky area where the grass was much taller.

"Too much action over there for me," commented Maggie. "You can make it to Samuel from here undetected. I might draw attention if I get closer."

Fred agreed and slid off Maggie's back into the tall grass. "Tomorrow morning just before sunrise, okay?"

"I'll be here," replied Maggie as he took flight.

Fred quickly made his way to the rock pile, but the entrance to Samuel's home was covered by a large bolder. It looked like the rocks had shifted. Fred called out, "Samuel, are you in there? Are you alright?"

"Fred, I'm over here in the tall grass-s-s."

Fred turned to see Samuel several feet away slithering through the tall grass towards the rock pile. "What happened?" asked Fred in a concerned voice.

"I was just getting into my morning routine of s-s-soaking up the s-s-sun's-s-s energy when the humans-s-s arrived with a big trailer," began Samuel as he moved closer. "The humans-s-s were backing up this-s-s long trailer when they ran into the rock pile, toppling s-s-several rocks-s-s from the top. I barely escaped the falling rocks-s-s. I made it to s-s-safety and decided to s-s-stay in the tall grass-s-s until the humans were finished. I think a huge rock s-s-smashed our flat rock for lying in the s-s-sun."

"What's going on?" interrupted Fred.

"We have a new visitor at the barn, Fred. A horse," answered Samuel.

Fred carefully walked around the rock pile to get a closer look at the humans. "It looks like they're on the back side of the barn taking care of the horse."

"I think we are s-s-safe for now," Samuel said softly. "Let's-s-s find a place to take in the s-s-sun and you can tell me about your trip to Frank's-s-s."

Shattered pieces of rock were everywhere. The shifting of the rock pile had caused several rocks at the top of the pile to fall and shatter as they met the ground. Samuel's thin body slinked between the remains of his previous sunning area. Just beyond that spot lay a new rock, bigger and much smoother, but slightly less flat. Samuel crawled to the top and called to Fred. "Over here my young friend. This-s-s s-s-spot will do nicely."

Fred crawled up and found a comfortable position next to Samuel. "S-s-so, Fred, what brings-s-s you back s-s-so s-s-soon? Did s-s-something happen that has you concerned?"

"Yes! Another mouse was there. A white mouse in a cage," replied Fred.

Fred proceeded to tell Samuel all about the encounter and how the white mouse refused to leave. "The mouse didn't want to be free. I don't understand."

"Follow me, and I will help you understand freedom," said Samuel as he slid off his rock and slithered towards the barn. Fred followed.

Samuel made his way to the back side of the barn where the humans were taking care of the new horse. He found a fence post with weeds growing around the base and he curled up next to it. Fred settled in next to Samuel. "Let's-s-s watch the humans-s-s for a while. They may show you the answer you s-s-seek. You can learn many lessons-s-s by watching other creatures-s-s of the world."

The two friends sat motionless watching the humans with the horse. One human was walking the horse around the pasture while the other was carrying a large bucket of water. The water kept spilling over the edge of the bucket as the human walked. The human with the bucket finally called to the other, "Just bring the horse over here."

Samuel turned to Fred. "Watch carefully," he said.

Fred sat watching intently, not sure what he was looking for. One human set the bucket of water down and the other led the horse over to the water. For a long minute the three, horse and two humans, stood quietly staring at the bucket. Then the humans tried to get the horse to take a drink by holding the bucket close to the horse's mouth. The horse refused and pulled away. Eventually, the humans set the bucket down and walked away. The horse stood looking at the bucket of water. Moments later he turned and walked away without taking a drink.

Samuel spoke. "Did you s-s-see that, Fred? The humans-s-s wanted to give the horse water, but the horse wasn't ready to take a drink and s-s-so it didn't accept the drink that was-s-s offered." Samuel paused for a moment to let Fred think and then added, "Fred, you can lead s-s-someone to freedom, but you cannot make them free. It is-s-s a choice. They have to want it." Samuel uncoiled his body and slithered towards his rock pile home. Fred followed.

Back on the rock Fred sat quietly soaking up the sun and contemplating Samuel's words. The day passed quickly and the sun was beginning to set when Fred finally spoke. "Samuel, I think I understand. Freedom means that one is free to make a choice. For example, you are free because you can choose to be a snake that does not eat meat. I am free because I can choose to be a mouse that is awake during the day and not at night like most mice. Frank is free because he can choose to be a field mouse or a house mouse."

"On the other hand, the white mouse is not free because she is limited by others. She cannot choose to stay or to leave. She cannot choose to eat berries and nuts instead of the food the humans leave for her. She cannot choose to run where she wants to run. Her choices are very limited and in some ways she has no choice at all."

"When one is truly free they have the choice to be who they desire to be without being limited by someone else."

Samuel smiled at Fred and calmly replied, "Yes-s-s."

"Then I know what I must do," said Fred, as he closed his eyes and took a smooth deep breath. "I have some lessons to teach someone about freedom."

Chapter 8

That Night

That night, while Fred curled up with Samuel in the snake's home under the rocks, Frank visited the white mouse once again. This time he came prepared. He brought with him blades of grass, a piece of a flower, nuts and berries from Fred's, bacon and eggs from earlier that morning, and a host of stories about what it is like outside the cage. If the white mouse did not know what is was like to be free, then Frank was determined to teach her the meaning of freedom.

"Psssst. Hello, white mouse," Frank called from on top of the cage.

The white mouse was running in a wire wheel in the middle of the cage and didn't notice Frank at first.

"Hey, mouse," Frank called louder.

Startled, she jumped from the wheel. "Oh, you scared me. I didn't think you were coming back."

"I didn't mean to startle you. I was just trying to get your attention. Allow me to introduce myself. I'm Frank. That was my cousin you were talking to earlier," said Frank. "I came to talk to you about getting out of the cage."

"I told your cousin that I'm fine right here and I don't want to leave," replied the white mouse.

"I thought I would share some of my world with you," said Frank, "so I brought some things from the outside."

He carefully slid several blades of grass through the tiny holes in the top of the cage. "Smell this. Taste it, too. It's called 'grass'. This is what covers most of the ground outside. In some places it grows really tall. It can grow 40 to 50 mouse-feet tall."

The white mouse sniffed carefully. "What do you do with it?"

"It serves a variety of purposes for us," replied Frank. "Certain types of grass we eat, other types are good for building our nests, and it's also great for hiding in and playing in."

"Here, smell this," continued Frank, as he pushed a piece of flower into the cage.

"Wow, that smells good," said the white mouse. "What is it?"

"That's a small part of a wildflower. Areas exist where these flowers cover the ground as far as a mouse can see. The air is filled with this beautiful smell," answered Frank.

"Now, here is some food. This is a piece of an acorn. This is a berry. And my favorite, bacon and eggs." Frank smiled as he forced bits of food through the tiny holes of the cage. "The humans in this house cook bacon and eggs every morning. That's why I decided to live in this house. I just love the taste of bacon and eggs."

The white mouse interrupted, "But I like the food I get and I don't have to go search for it everyday. The humans bring me more whenever I need it."

Frank thought for a moment, not sure how to reply. "Let me tell you about some of my experiences and what it is like for me to be free." He paused. "Just last week I learned to fly."

"What do you mean you learned to fly?" she questioned.

"Well, I didn't really fly myself, but I soared through the air on the back of a bird. I felt the wind blowing through my fur and my whiskers tingle as the air rushed passed my face. From high in the sky I could see for miles." Frank sighed as he remembered that special feeling.

"Last week was filled with many new experiences. Not only did I fly but I also met a snake and sat in the sun with him. We talked together and I learned how to listen to my inner feelings," continued Frank.

The white mouse was amazed to hear that Frank knew a snake and even talked to it.

She had always been told how dangerous they were and to stay away from them.

Frank talked with the white mouse for the rest of the evening about where he was born and about his family. He shared everything about growing up as a field mouse and life as he knew it outside.

The night passed quickly for the two mice, and soon daylight began to break.

Realizing that he was supposed to meet Fred at first light, Frank excused himself and headed for the crack in the wall. He hoped his evening with the white mouse helped her to better understand freedom. Frank hurried to meet Fred.

Chapter 9

The Choice

Frank was waiting at the base of the house when Fred arrived. "The humans are still asleep. This is a good time to go rescue the white mouse," Frank told Fred.

This time Fred led the way into the crack, up the inside of the wall, over the pots and pans, across the kitchen floor, and up the side of the couch. Frank kept pace with Fred, and within moments the two cousins were standing opposite the white mouse. She was sleeping in the corner of the glass cage.

"Together we can chew a hole in that top

section," said Fred. "The rest is up to her."

As the two began chewing, the white mouse woke. "What are you doing?" she asked.

Fred quickly spoke up while Frank continued chewing. "We are offering you a choice. Once we have finished chewing a hole, you can choose to use it or not. We can only offer you freedom and a chance to be out of that cage. You have to decide to climb to the top and pull yourself out. We cannot make you free. You have to take the final step to free yourself."

"But the only thing I know about life outside this cage is what Frank told me last night. I know life in here," interrupted the white mouse.

"We will help you once you are out. We'll show you how to build a nest and how to scurry and scamper in the field, where to find the best-tasting berries, and how to avoid danger," replied Fred.

"I don't know if I can do it," she replied timidly.

"And you won't know until you take the next step," said Fred encouragingly. "Freedom is about having a choice. My cousin and I will give you the choice. The next step is up to you."

Fred returned to gnawing on the thin metal that covered the glass cage while the white mouse watched intently from below. An hour had passed when finally a chunk of metal fell into the cage. The hole was done. Fred stuck his head inside and in a gentle voice said, "We chewed a hole directly above this hanging water bottle. You can climb up the side of the bottle and slide right out. Now you have the choice to be free or not. For once in your life you have freedom. You are free to choose. You decide. We'll wait on the floor for you as long as we can."

Fred and Frank quickly jumped from the top and worked their way to the floor.

They found a spot out of sight of the humans and they waited.

Soon the house became filled with the noise of the humans. "Eating time will begin soon," said Frank, smiling. "Every morning, bacon and eggs. I love it!"

Frank was right. The scene that Fred had witnessed a day earlier began to unfold before his eyes. First a bunch of commotion in the kitchen and then that wonderful smell, followed by the thrashing of hands and arms as the humans ate, and finally the gathering of the food from under the table as the humans went about their day.

The food was certainly delicious, but it did not help Fred's feelings of sadness.

The white mouse did not come out of her cage.

The day passed, and Fred decided to leave. "I'll keep an eye on her," said Frank. "Maybe she will be ready at another time and we can offer her more freedom then."

Fred nodded to Frank and said, "Let me know if she changes her mind." As Fred slipped through the crack, he looked back at Frank. "Take care of yourself, my house mouse cousin. I'll let everyone know you're happy and doing well."

And then, in the faint distance, Frank heard, "I'll come back whenever she's ready."

Chapter 10

One Month Later

 One month later Fred was sitting with Samuel in the afternoon sun, as was their custom. Fred sighed.

"What's-s-s bothering you, Fred?" asked Samuel calmly.

"I feel sad. A month has passed and the white mouse has not chosen to come out of her cage," said Fred. "I wanted her to be free."

"Fred," said Samuel gently. "She was free. Freedom was not about being out of the cage. It was about having the opportunity to choose. The white mouse had the choice to s-s-stay in the cage or to leave, just as Frank had the choice to s-s-stay outside as a field mouse or to move inside and become a house mouse. Frank is-s-s not trapped in the house because he

chooses-s-s to be there. In a s-s-similar way, the white mouse is-s-s not trapped in the cage because she chooses-s-s to be there. Remember, freedom is-s-s about having a choice. You gave the white mouse the choice. She exercised her freedom and chose to s-s-stay."

Fred looked at Samuel and replied, "If she ever decides that she wants to leave, I will give her that choice again."

Samuel nodded his head in approval and smiled.

Mice
And others
From

FRED
The Mouse™
Rescuing Freedom

FRED: The mouse scurry and scamper champion from Book One: The Adventures Begin and Book Two: Making Friends. Not only is he the fastest mouse ever seen at the Mouse Scurry and Scamper School, he also has a unique ability of trusting his intuition.

FRANK: A field mouse who is Fred's cousin.

SAMUEL: A wise old garter snake who lives under a rock pile near Fred's home.

THE WHITE STRANGER: An albino mouse that Frank and Fred discover in a cage in the humans' house.

LOU: A barn swallow who lives in a nest at the peak of the new barn that Fred calls home. He lives with his best friend, Lou.

LOU: Like his best friend, Lou, he too is a barn swallow. The two birds live in a nest at the peak of the new barn.

MAGGIE: A large crow who is the leader of the "Mob of Crows."

TIFFANY: The human family's golden retriever watchdog.

MR. MORTENSEN: An old gray mouse, the principal at the Mouse Scurry and Scamper School.

BRITTNEY ANNE: A niece of Fred. She is a young field mouse who has a tendency to whine like her mother, Brittney.

ABOUT THE AUTHOR
Reese Haller

Portraits by Gregg

Reese is nine years old and a fifth grader at Kolb Elementary in Bay City, Michigan. He is considered one of the youngest published fiction authors in America. He began writing short stories in Kindergarten where he was encouraged to take risks with his writing. He discovered his joy and passion in the third grade where he blossomed as a writer.

While at the age of eight, before entering fourth grade, Reese wrote his first book *Fred The Mouse™ Book One: The Adventures Begin.* It is a Benjamin Franklin Award silver medal winner. He wrote *Fred the Mouse™ Book Two: Making Friends* during his Christmas break in December 2005. Reese wrote *Fred the Mouse™ Book Three: Rescuing Freedom* during the summer before entering 5th grade. For more information visit Reese at <u>www.reesehaller.com</u>.

Reese is a regular presenter at elementary schools across the country where he lectures on the 6 traits of writing in a captivating 45 minute presentation. He has presented live to over 15,000 people in teacher in-services, keynote addresses and numerous elementary classrooms discussing writing and publishing. Reese has appeared live on The Martha Stewart Show reaching thousands with his message about writing and reading.

On March 19, 2006, Reese was appointed the Ambassador of Literacy for the Youth of Michigan by Michigan's Governor Jennifer Granholm.

Reese lives on an Equine Retirement and Rescue Ranch in Michigan with his parents and younger brother. To make a tax deductible donation visit www.healingacres.com.

Reese's dad is an author of parenting books and a couples and child therapist who lectures frequently on raising responsible, caring, confident children. He also writes a free monthly newsletter for parents and one for teachers. Visit him at www.thomashaller.com.

Reese's mom is a kindergarten teacher in the public schools where she has taught for over 17 years. His brother Parker, age 6, enjoys rescuing bugs and playing the drums.

ABOUT THE ILLUSTRATOR

Thomas Haller
M.Div., LMSW, ACSW, DST

Portraits by Gregg

Lynne Galsterer, the illustrator of *Fred the Mouse™ Book One and Book Two*, was unable to draw the pictures for *Fred the Mouse™ Book Three: Rescuing Freedom*. We wish to thank Lynne for all her hard work in creating the original look of Fred and all the characters. We honor her for giving us a clear portrayal of what Reese envisioned as he wrote about Fred's adventures.

Following Lynne's design, Reese's dad, Thomas Haller stepped in to put his hand to the test.

This is Thomas' first illustrative effort. As the author of several books he found a new appreciation for illustrators of children's books.

Thomas is a widely sought after national and international presenter in the areas of child behavior management and verbal language skills. He is the founder and director of Healing Minds Institute, a center devoted to teaching others to focus and enhance the health of the mind, body, and spirit. He is also the president of Personal Power Press, Inc., a printing company devoted to providing parents and teachers with effective resources for managing children's behavior. You can see their dynamic resources at www.personalpowerpress.com.

Thomas has maintained a private practice for 18 years in Bay City, Michigan, as a child, adolescent and couples therapist; a certified sex therapist; and a chronic pain counselor.

Visit Thomas at www.thomashaller.com.

 # Reese's Charity

I am donating a portion of the proceeds from my *Fred the Mouse*™ Book Series to **Healing Acres Equine Retirement Ranch, Inc.,** for the purpose of establishing a reading library at the ranch.

My goal is to create a library and maintain a reading program at **Healing Acres** where children have the opportunity to read with a horse or about a horse while they are visiting the ranch. I envision a place where children can read about how to care for a horse and then have a chance to touch, brush, feed, and even ride a real horse. I chose a wall in the barn that I want to turn into bookshelves so people have a variety of reading choices about horses.

As a way to remember their experience, I will give to every visitor, young and old, a book about horses to take home.

I want every child to have the opportunity to experience the same joy I experience every day: the joy of reading and the joy of being with horses.

If you wish to make a donation beyond the purchase of this book, please visit: www.healingacres.com.

Thank you for helping me create my dream.

HOW TO INVITE REESE TO YOUR SCHOOL

Would you like Reese to come to your school for a Literacy Day?

It's easy. Just e-mail Reese at reese@reesehaller.com and ask about available dates for a Literacy Day.

You can also call Personal Power Press toll-free at **877-360-1477** and ask about scheduling Reese for a Literacy Day.

When you schedule a Literacy Day, your school receives:

• Reese for the entire day presenting the 6 Traits of Writing and talking about his love of reading and writing.
• Signed copies of *Fred the Mouse*™ books
• A parent evening workshop where Reese and his dad give parents practical strategies and fun exercises that will inspire a love of writing in children.

INVITE REESE TODAY!!
www.reesehaller.com